For information regarding permissions, please write to:
Too Much Fun, LLC 1178 Farnsworth Rd. Waterville, OH 43566 U.S.A.
info@carruthstudio.com

Publisher's Cataloging-in-Publication Data
Carruth, George Albert.
What Stinks? / by George Carruth; illustrations by Libby Carruth Krock.
p. cm.
ISBN 978-0-9773167-2-4
Summary: A young boy and girl try to locate a bad smell in their house.
The harder they look, the dirtier and stinkier they become.

[1. Body, Human--Fiction. 2. Stories in rhyme.]
I. Krock, Libby Carruth. II. Title.

PZ7.C19248. W4 2007
[E]--dc22 2007923644
Printed in China
First printing, March 2007

What Stinks?

by George Carruth
illustrations by Libby Carruth Krock

Too Much Fun, LLC   Eastsound, WA

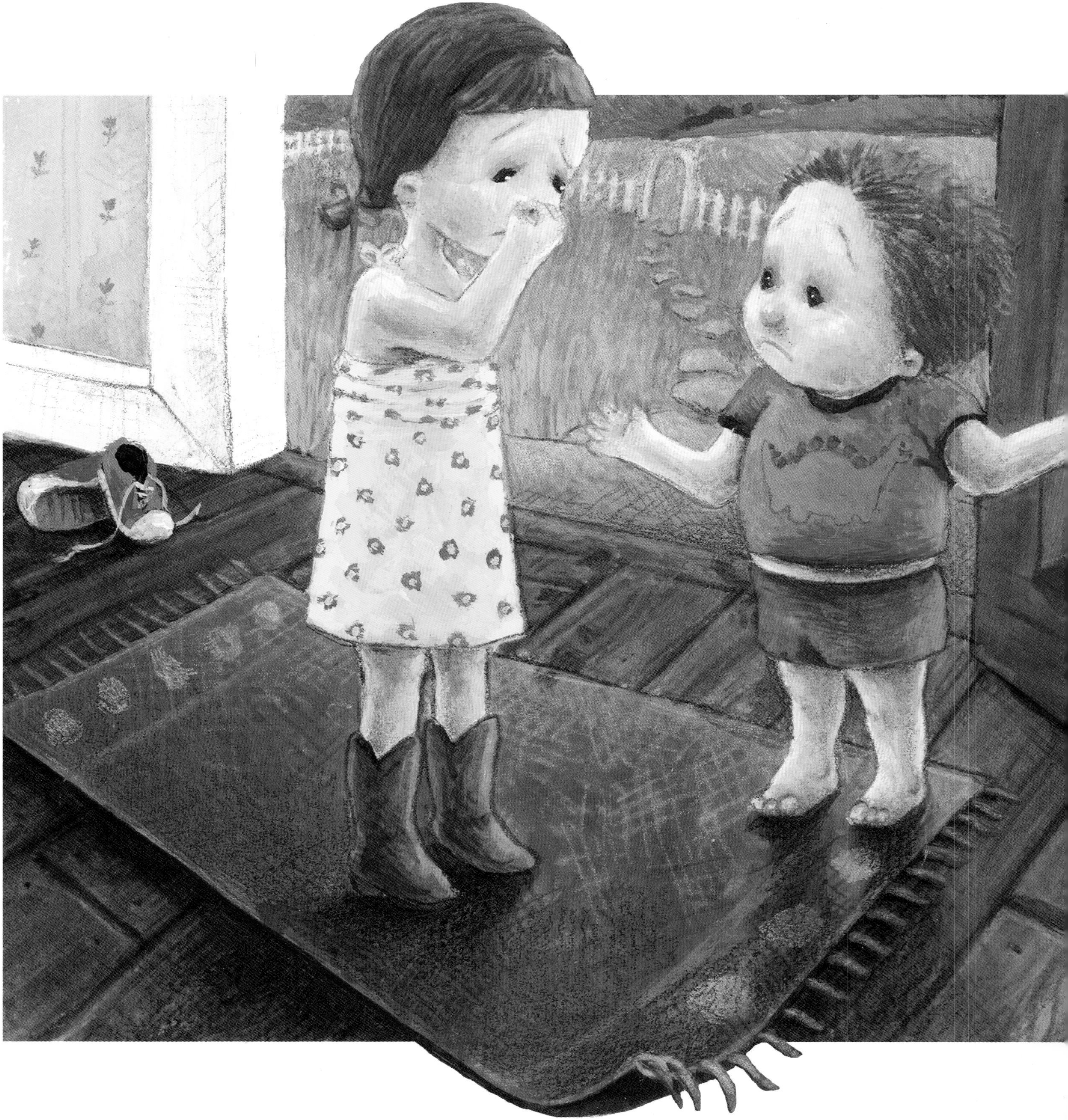

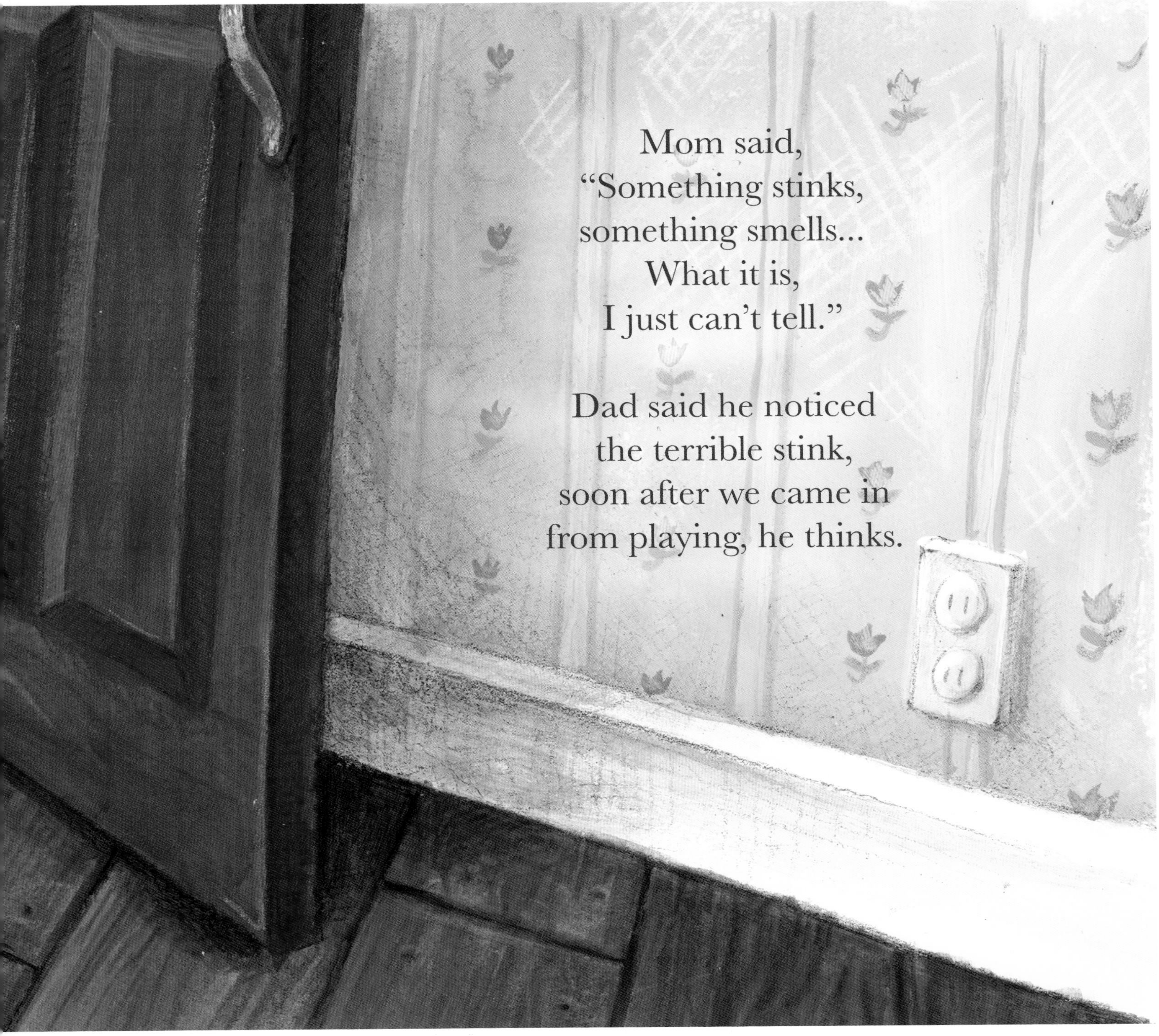
Mom said,
“Something stinks,
something smells...
What it is,
I just can’t tell.”

Dad said he noticed
the terrible stink,
soon after we came in
from playing, he thinks.

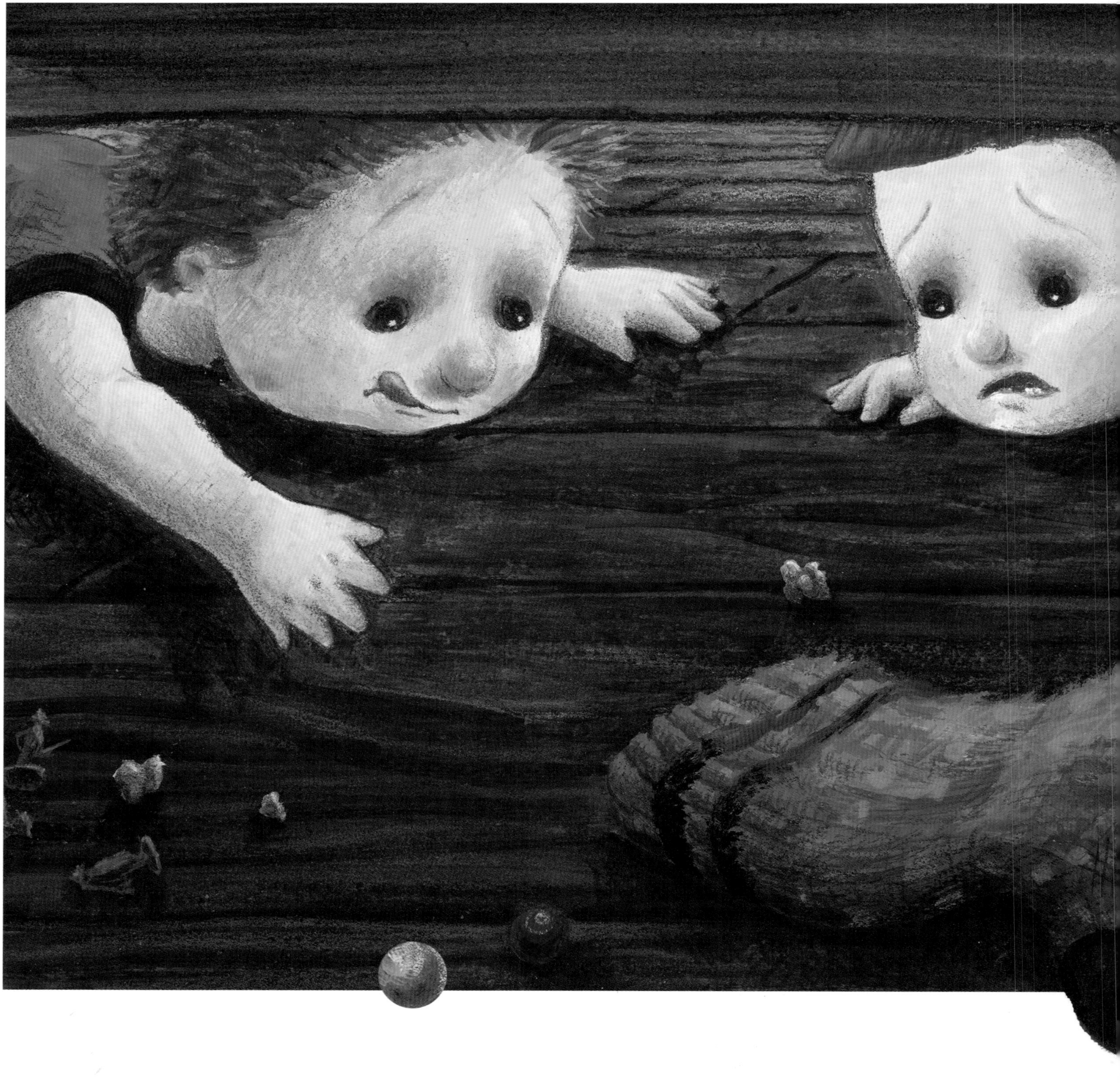

Someone said,
"Check under the bed!"

We looked and found
this fuzzy sock.
Is **this** what smells?
No, it's not.

We thought we'd look
inside the closet.

It's someone's lunch!
Who could've lost it?

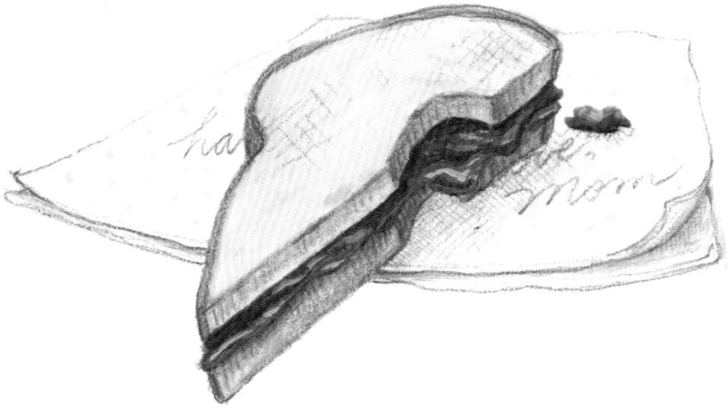
mom

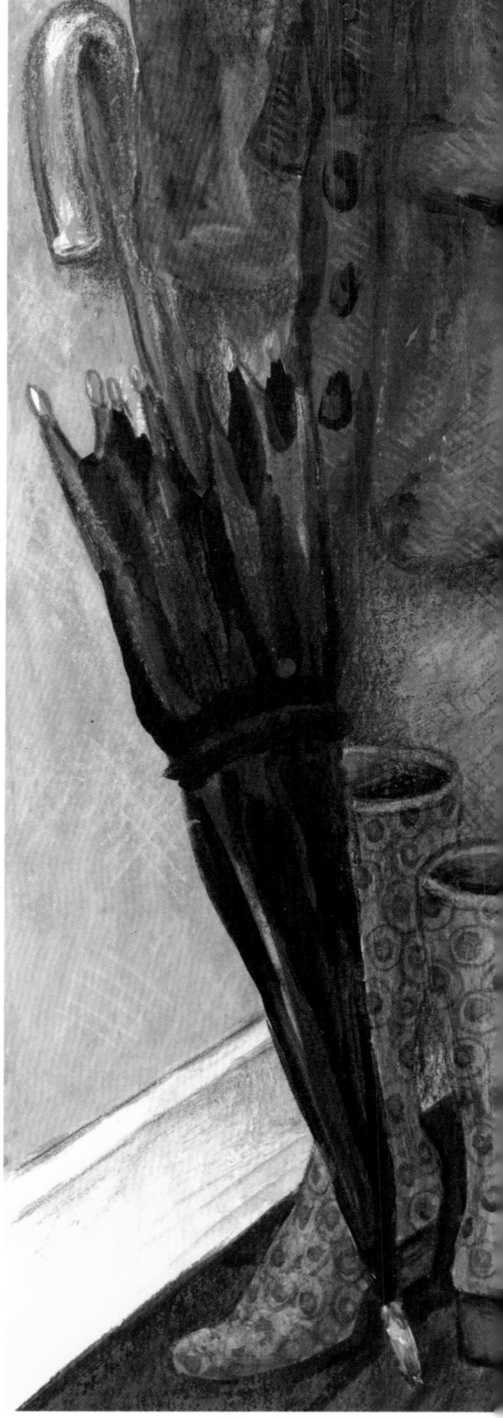

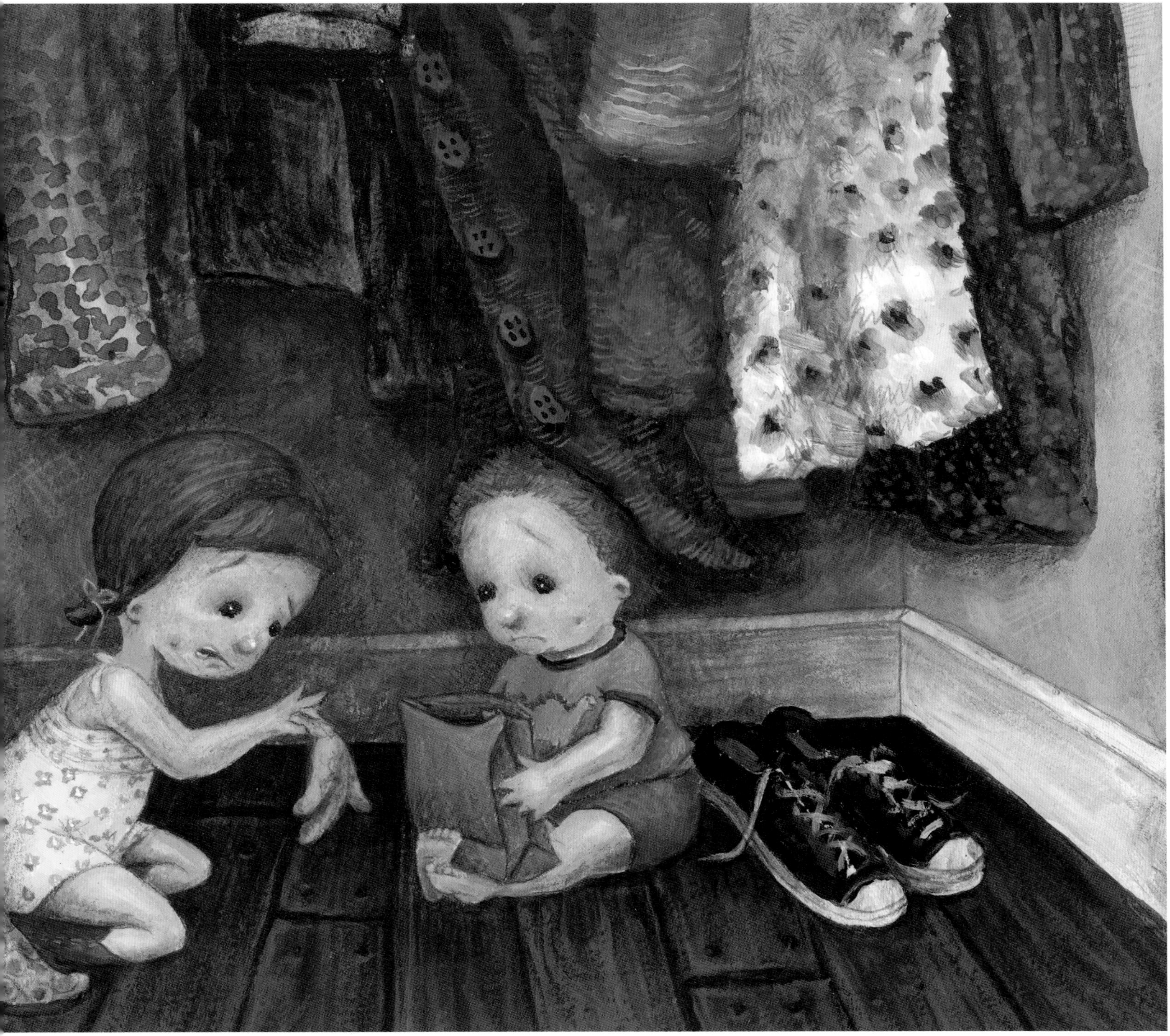

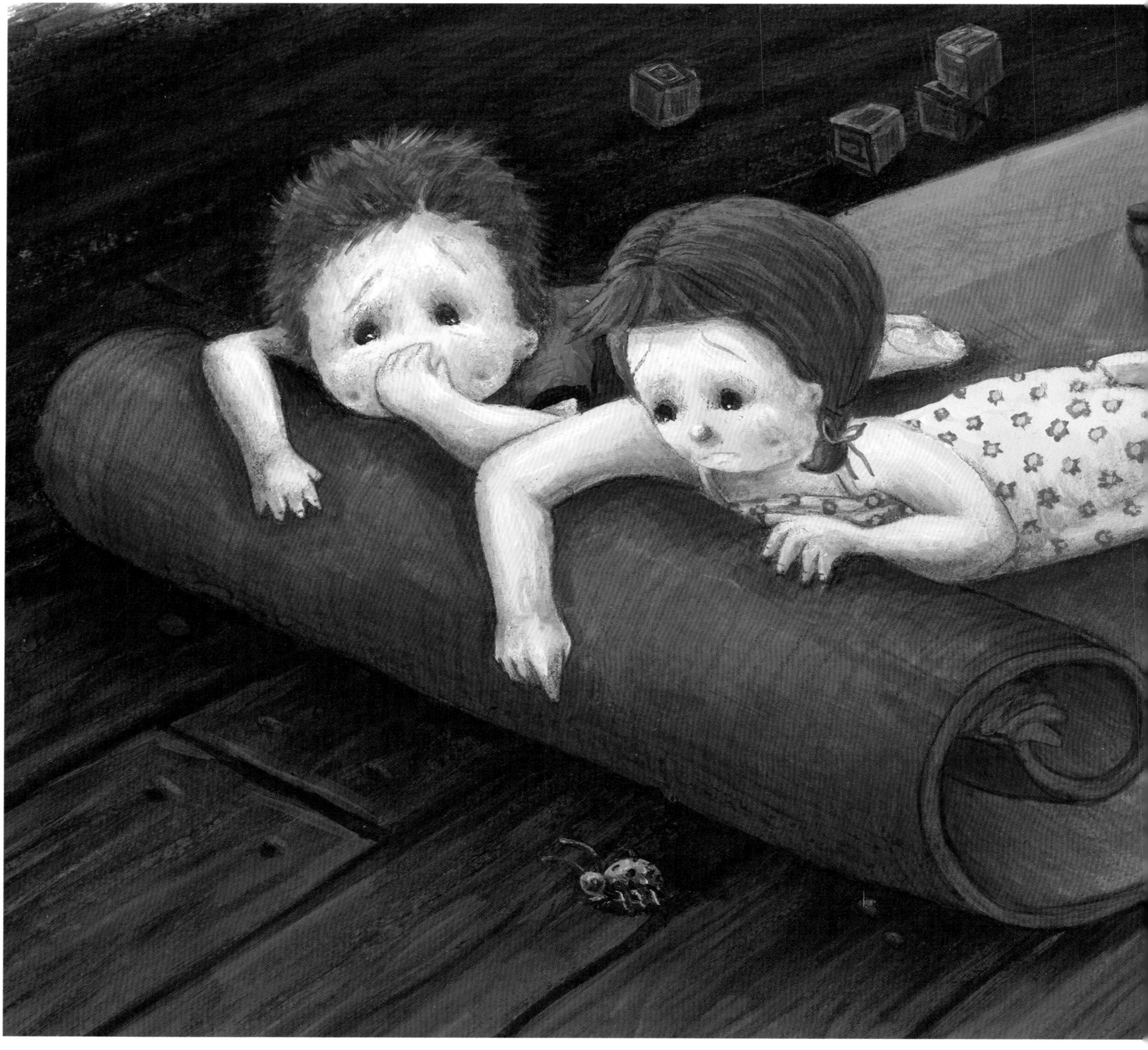

That smell might be coming
from under the rug.

It smells kind of funny,
but it's not **_this_** bug.

We should probably check
the entire house!

It might be a rat,
but it's not **this** mouse!

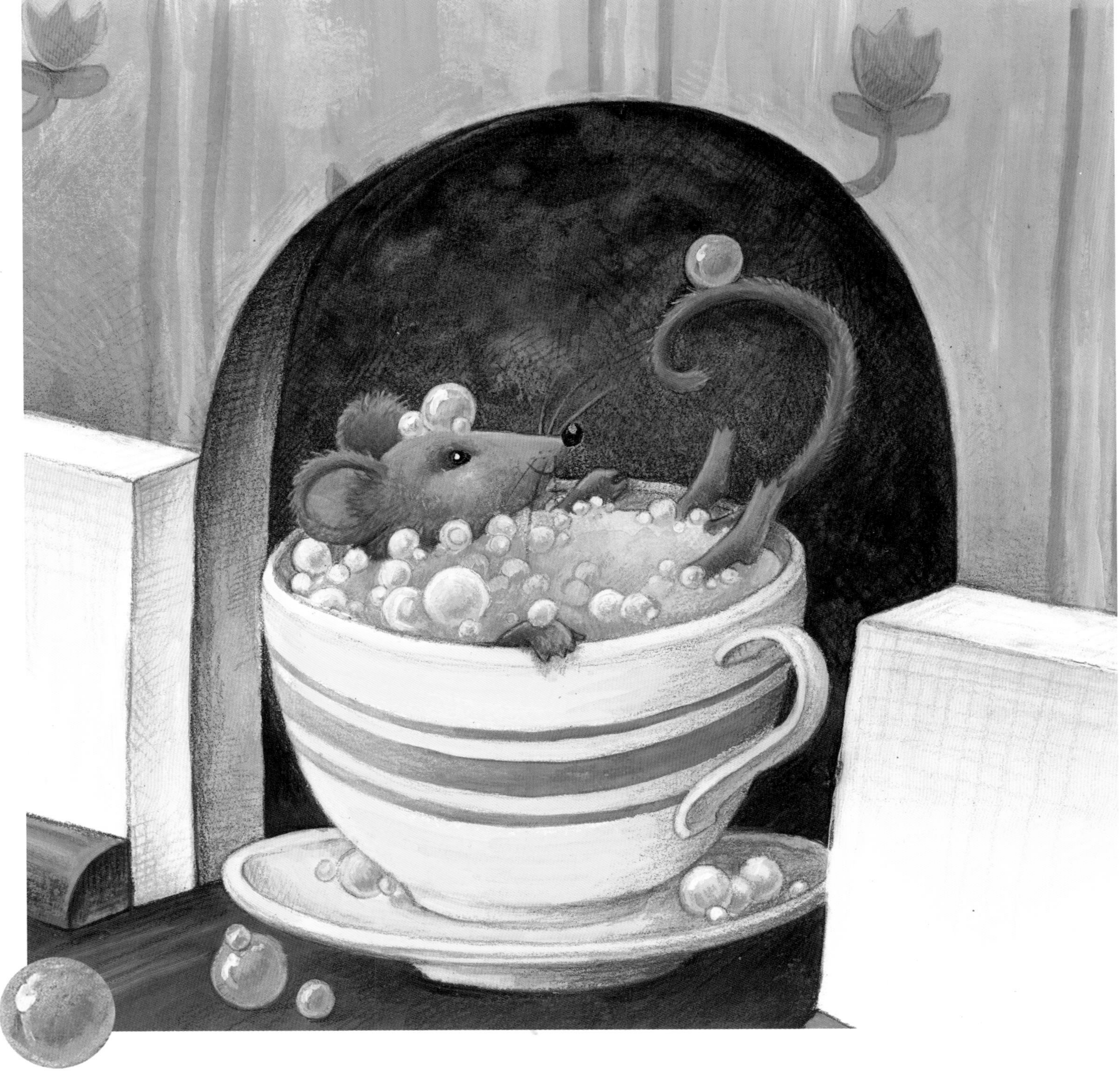

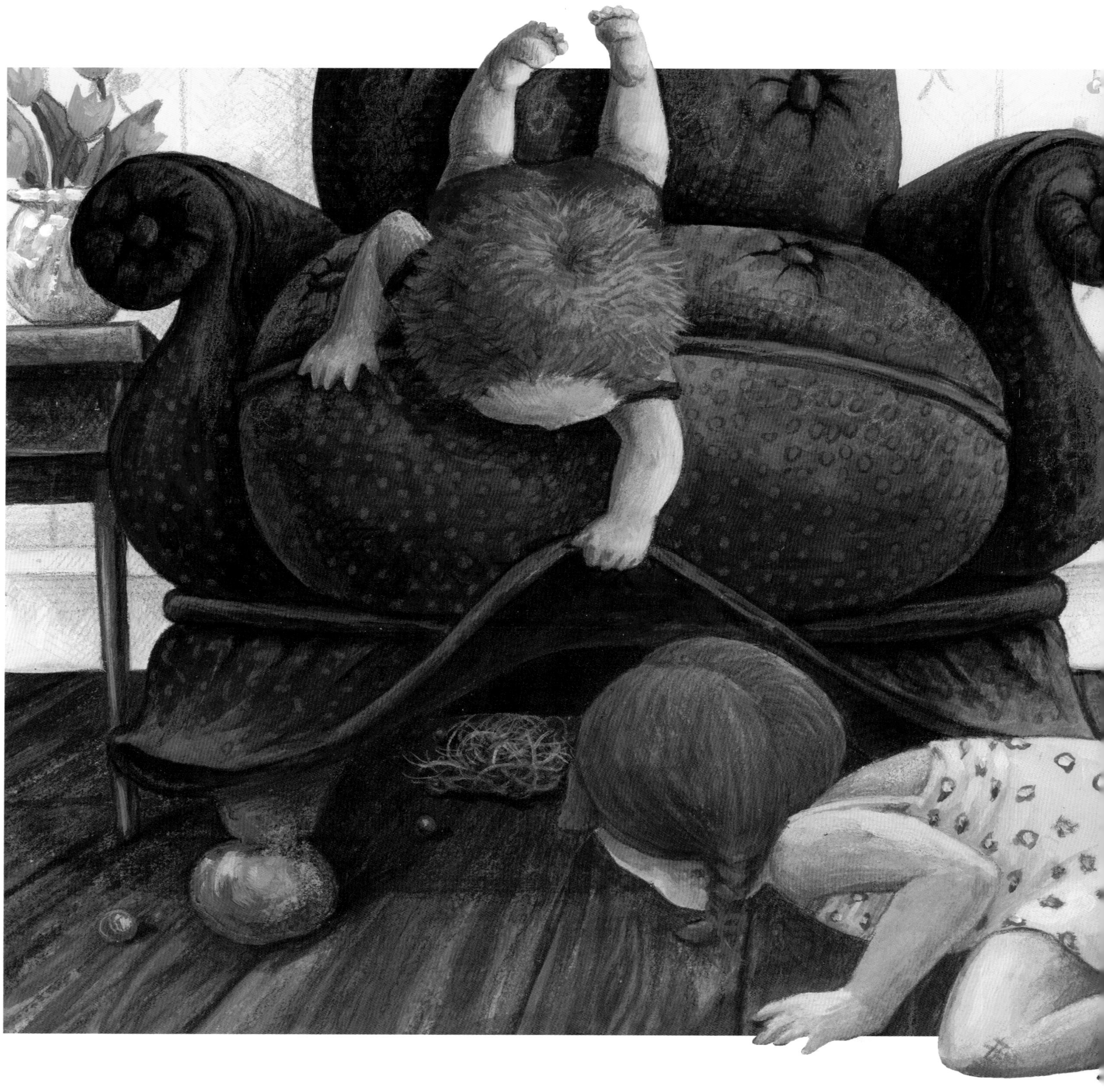

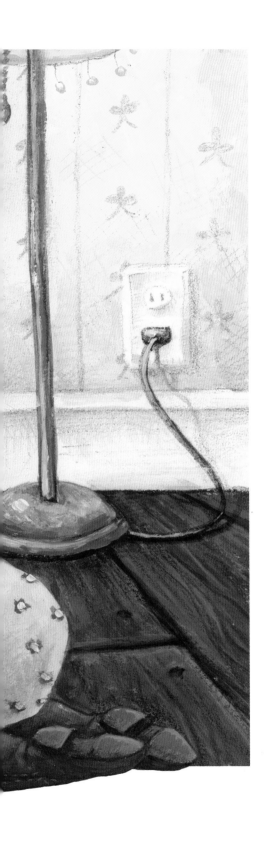

Maybe it's coming
from under the chair.

Look at the size
of that ball of hair!

It may be coming
from under the sink.

It's dark and damp
but doesn't stink.

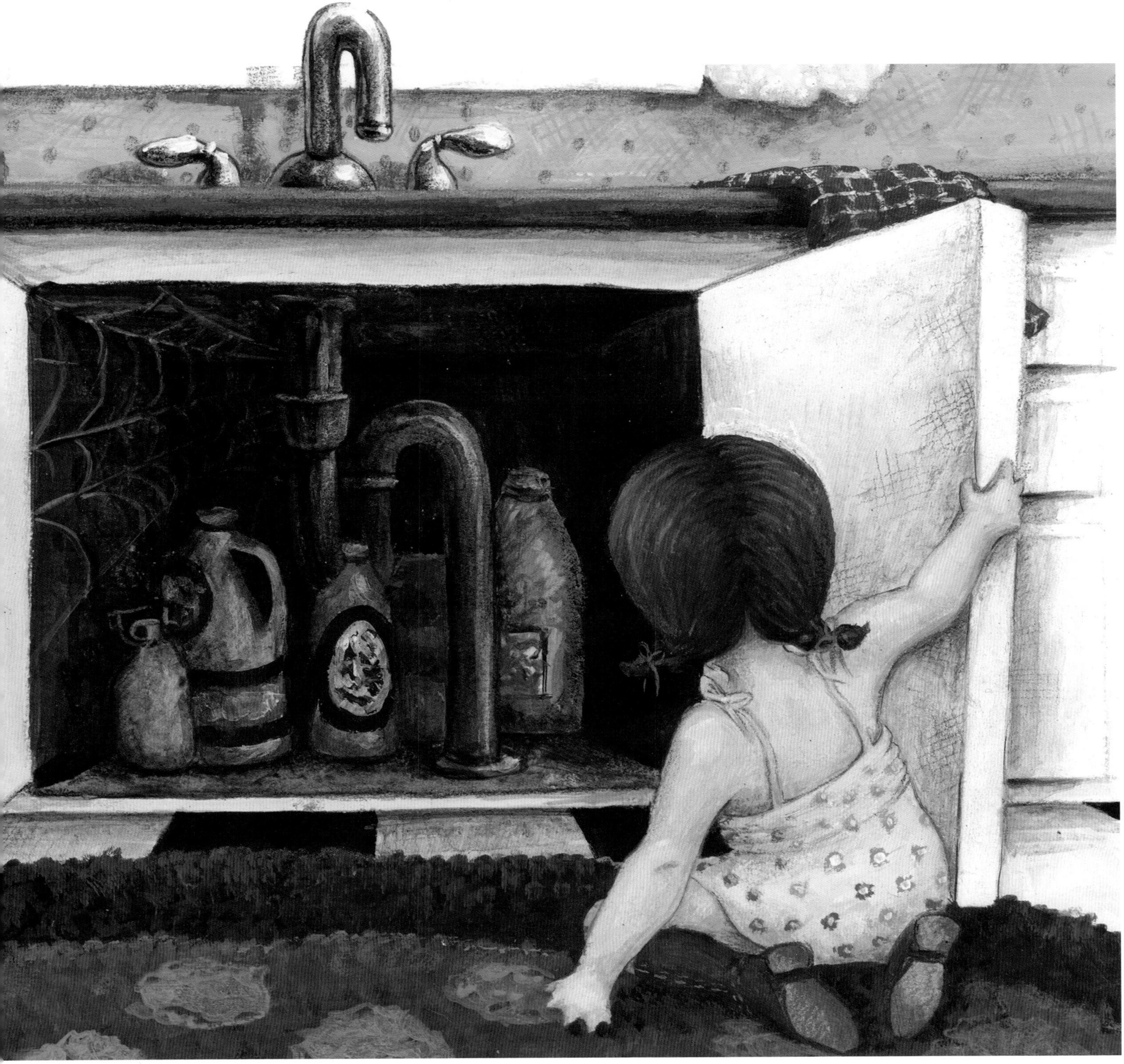

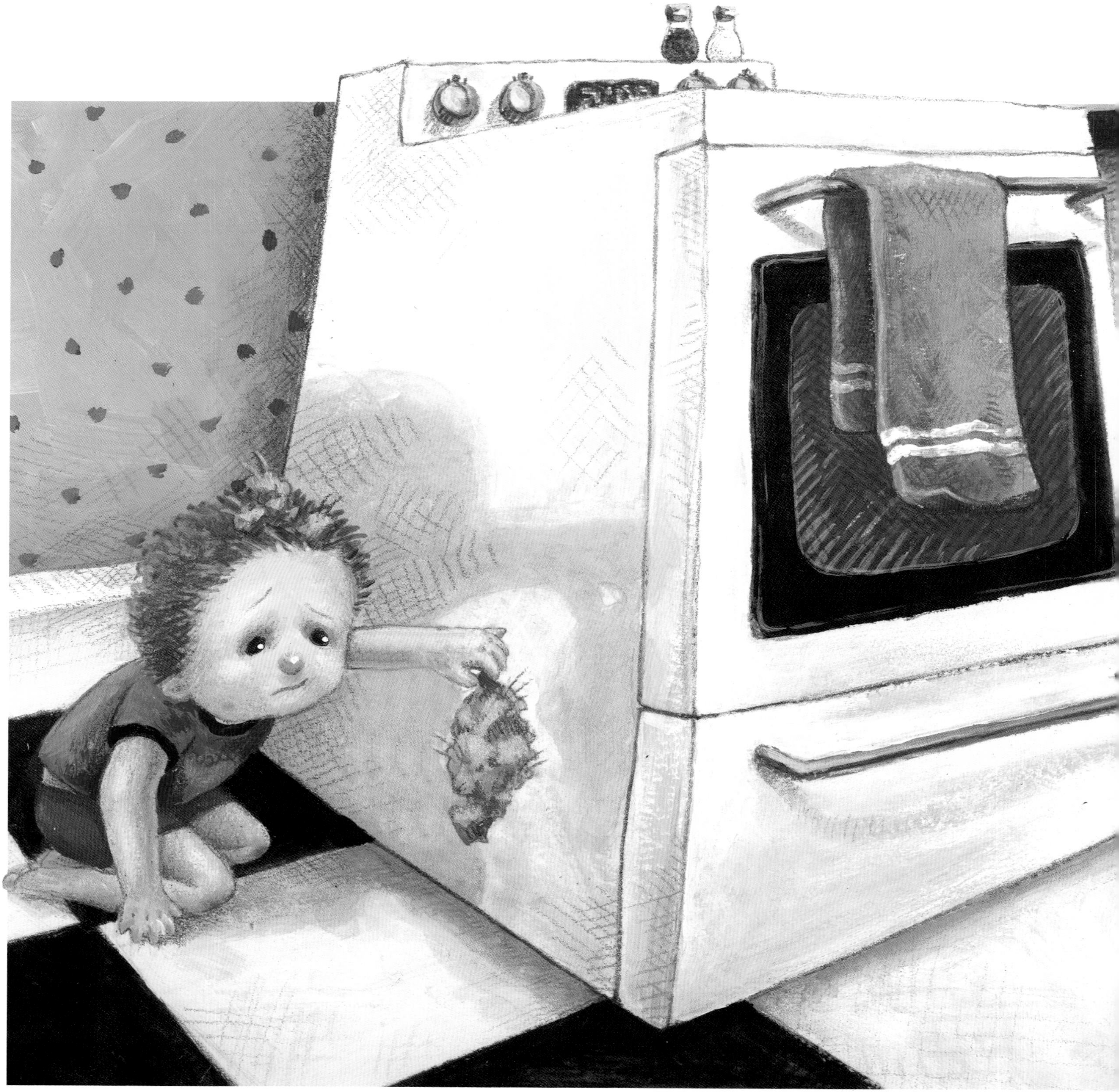

Maybe we'll check
under the stove.
What this was,
we'll never know!

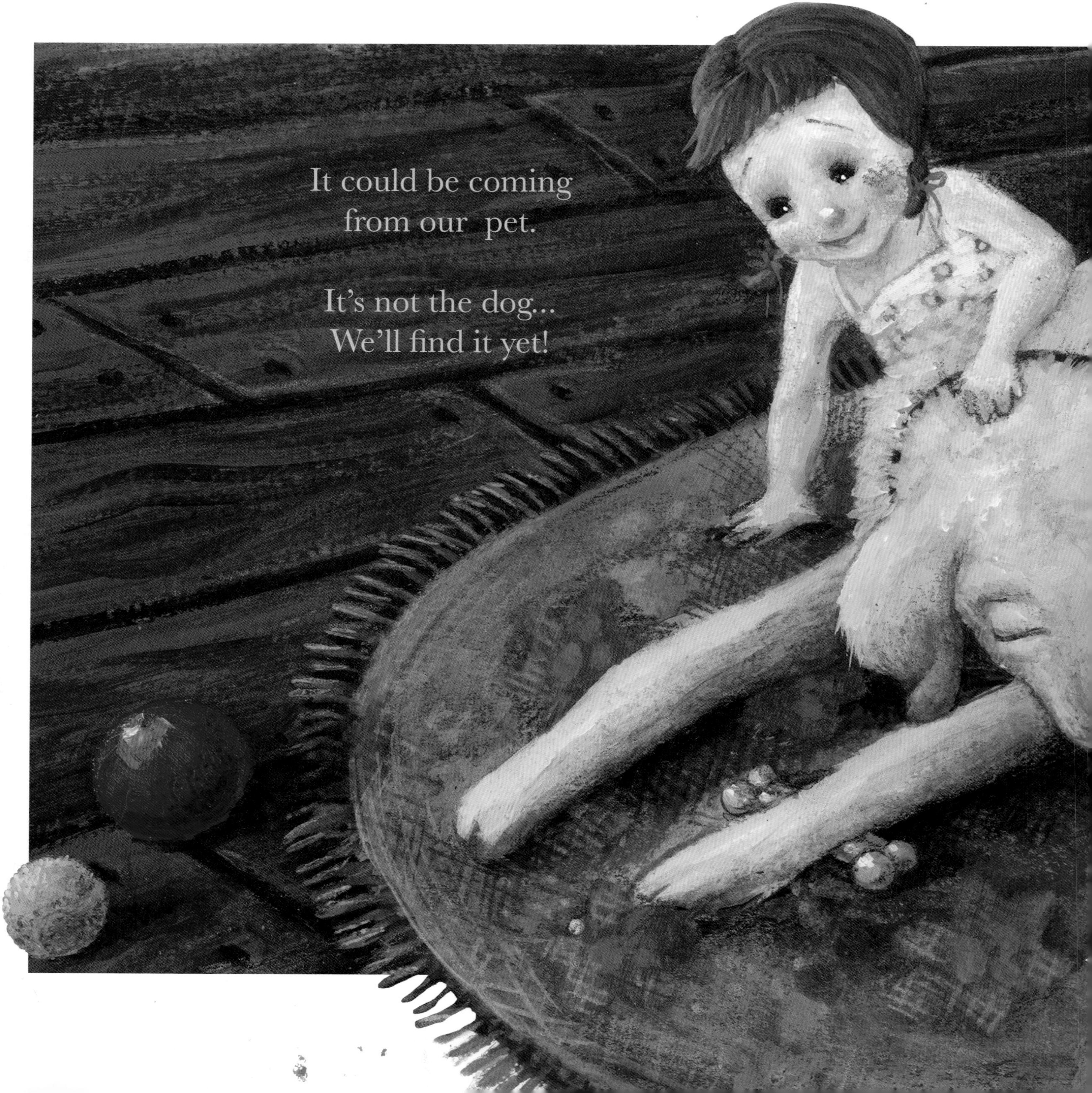
It could be coming
from our pet.

It's not the dog...
We'll find it yet!

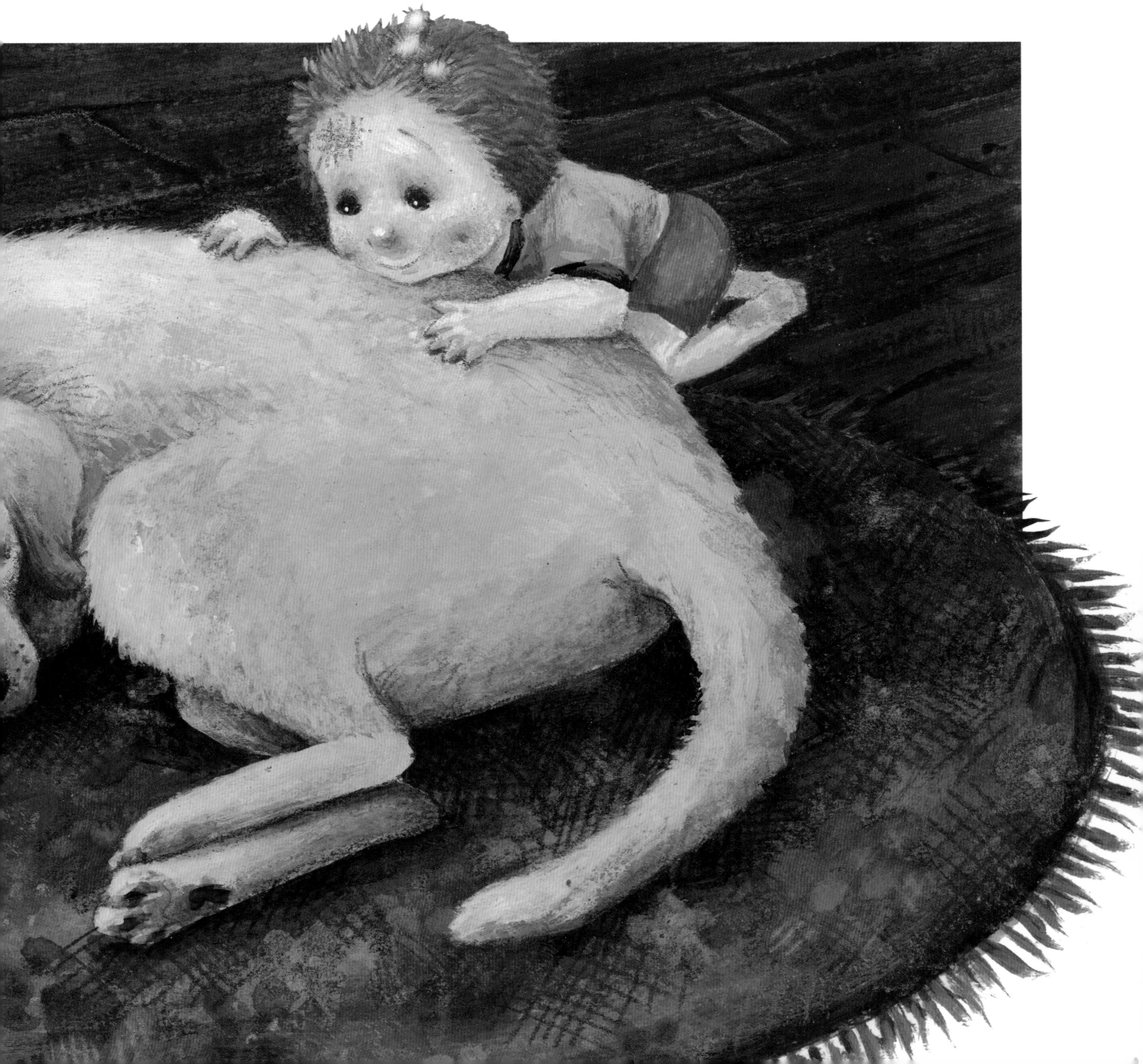

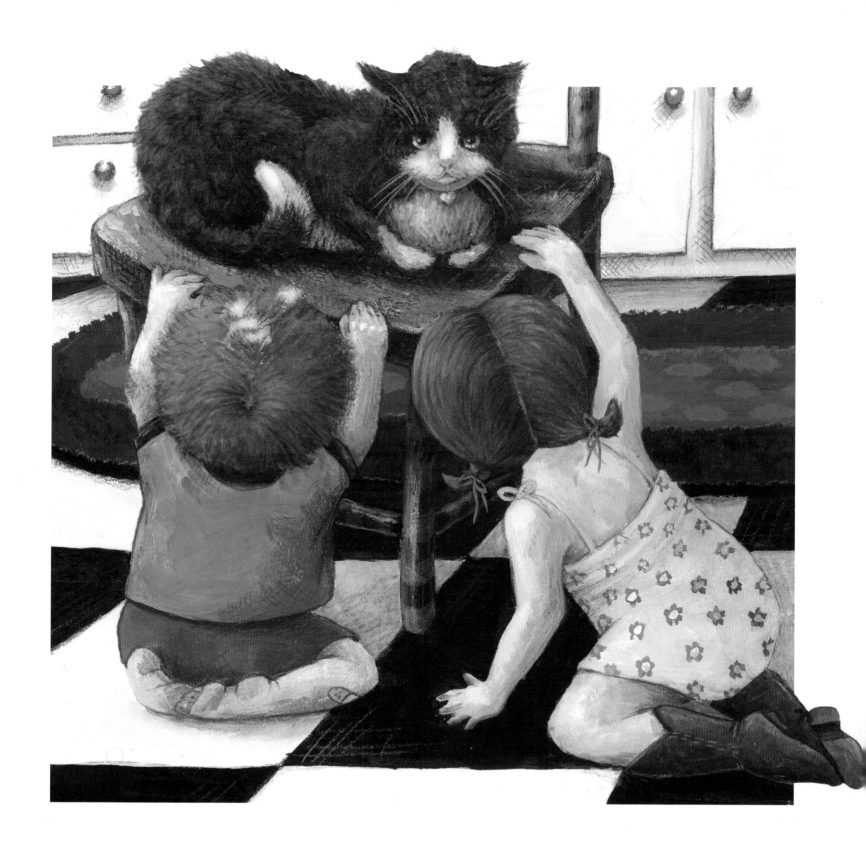

We thought for sure
it was the cat!

She smells ok.
Sorry about that!

To find that smell,
Mom and Dad were asked...
They looked at each other
and began to laugh!

Mom giggled quietly,
Dad belly-laughed.
They then shouted loudly,
"You both need a bath!"

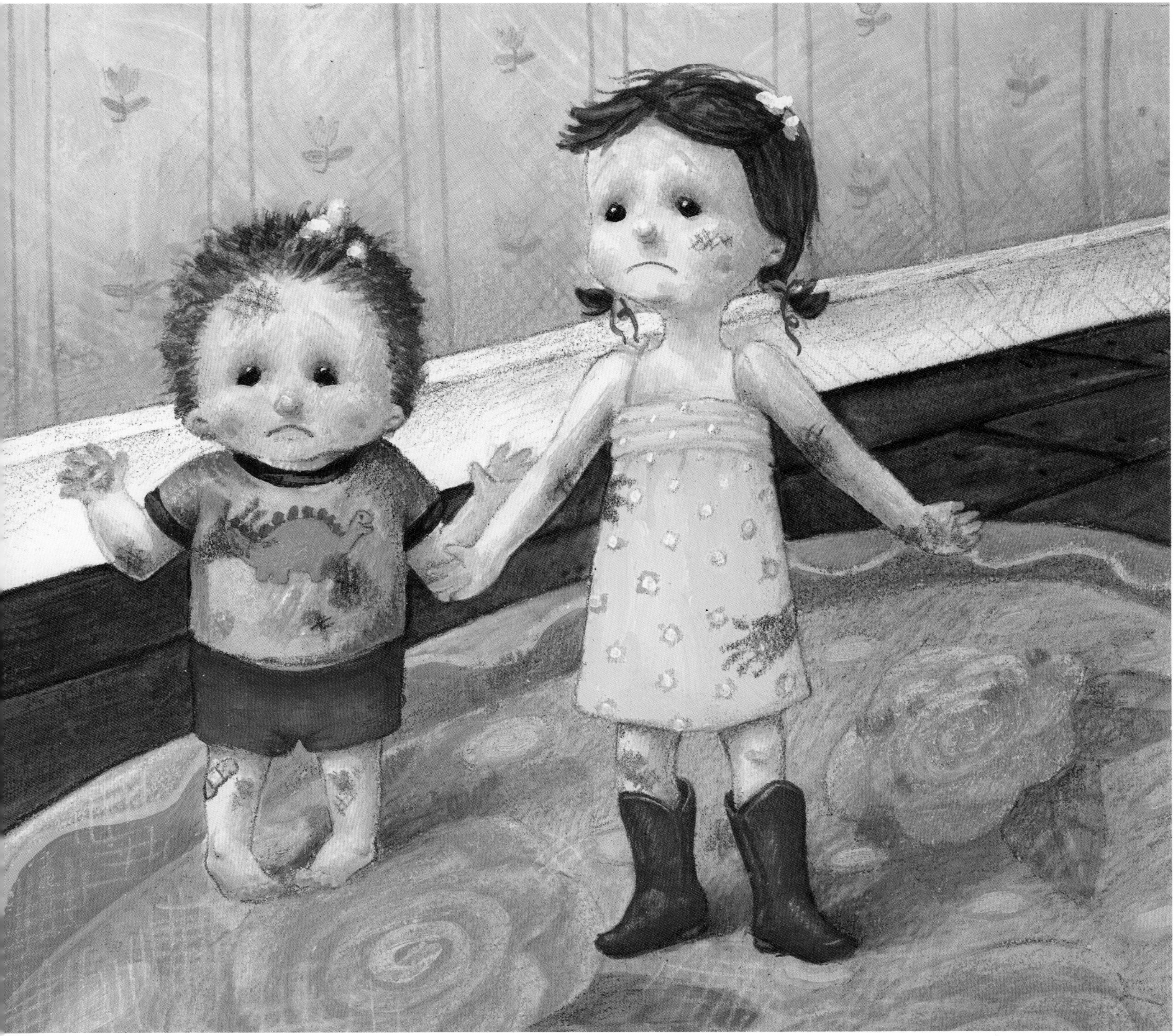

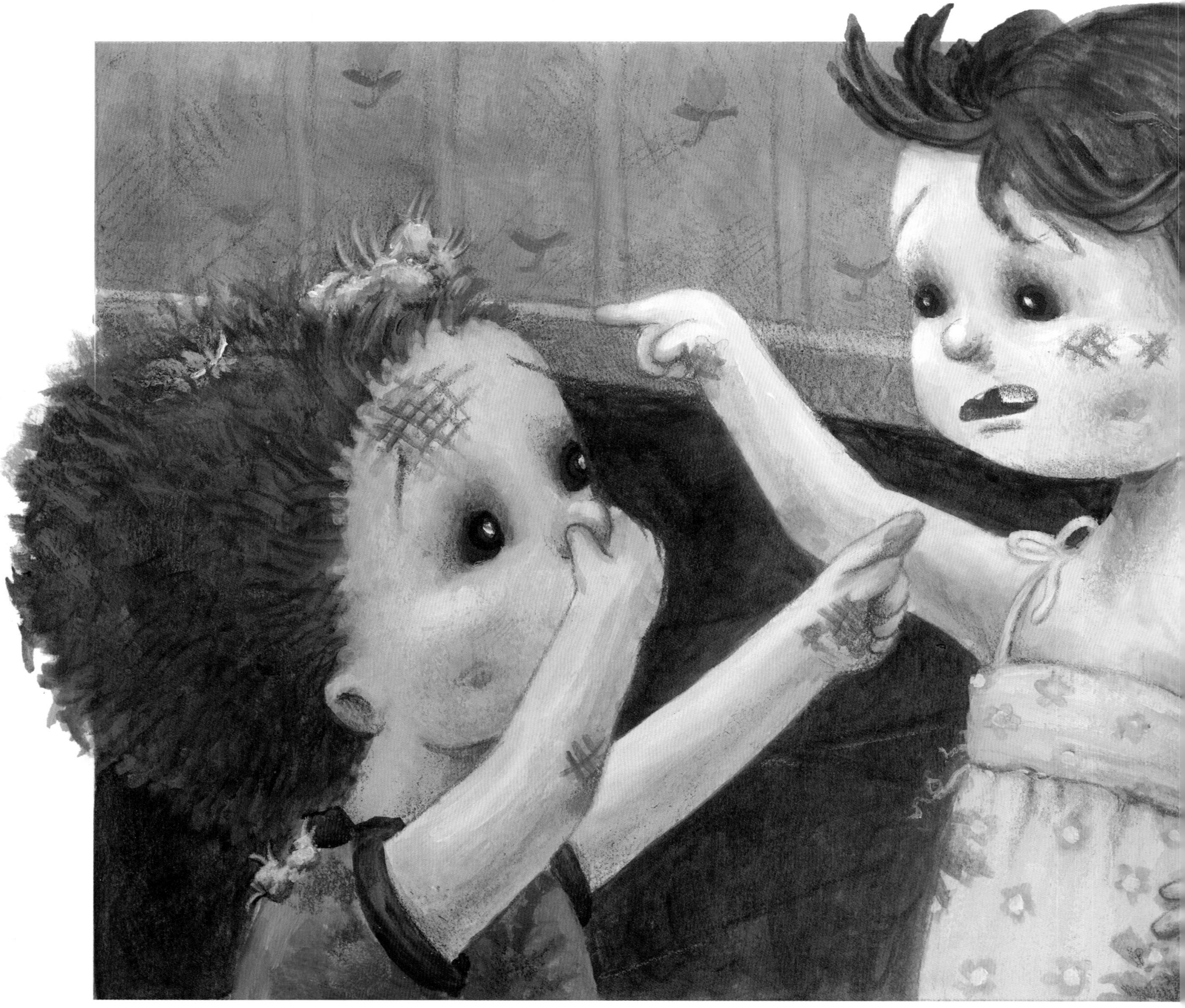

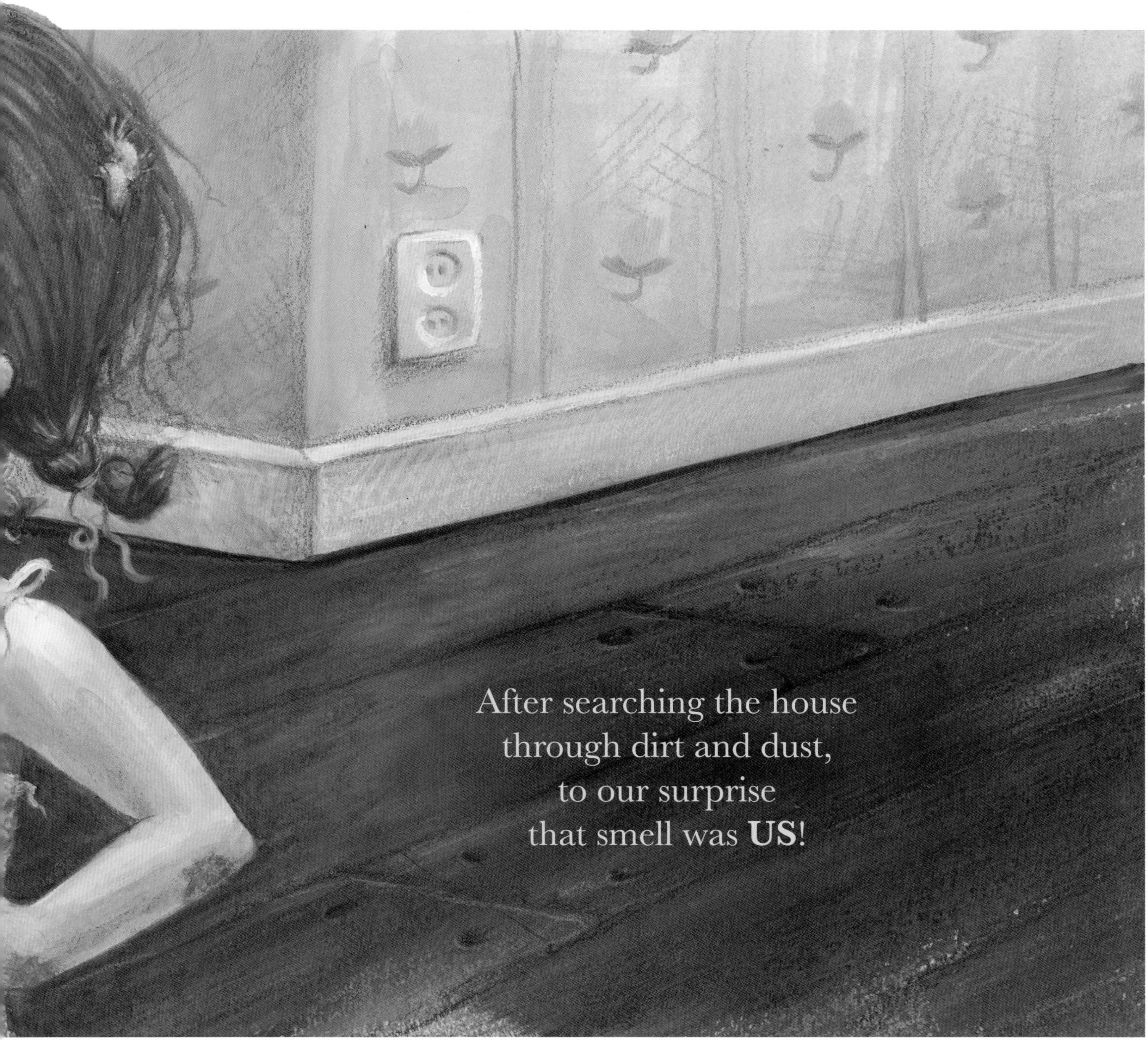
After searching the house
through dirt and dust,
to our surprise
that smell was **US**!

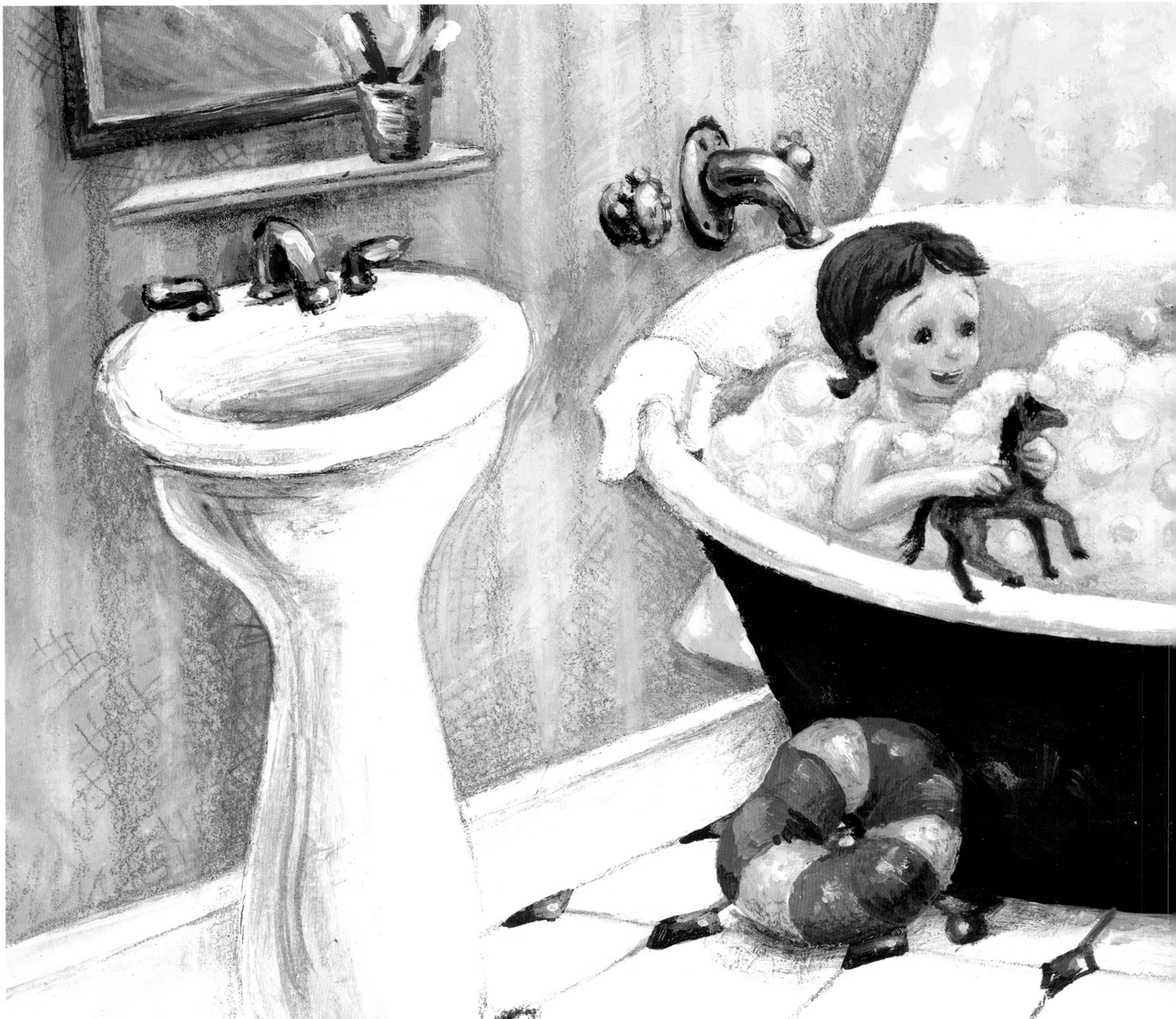

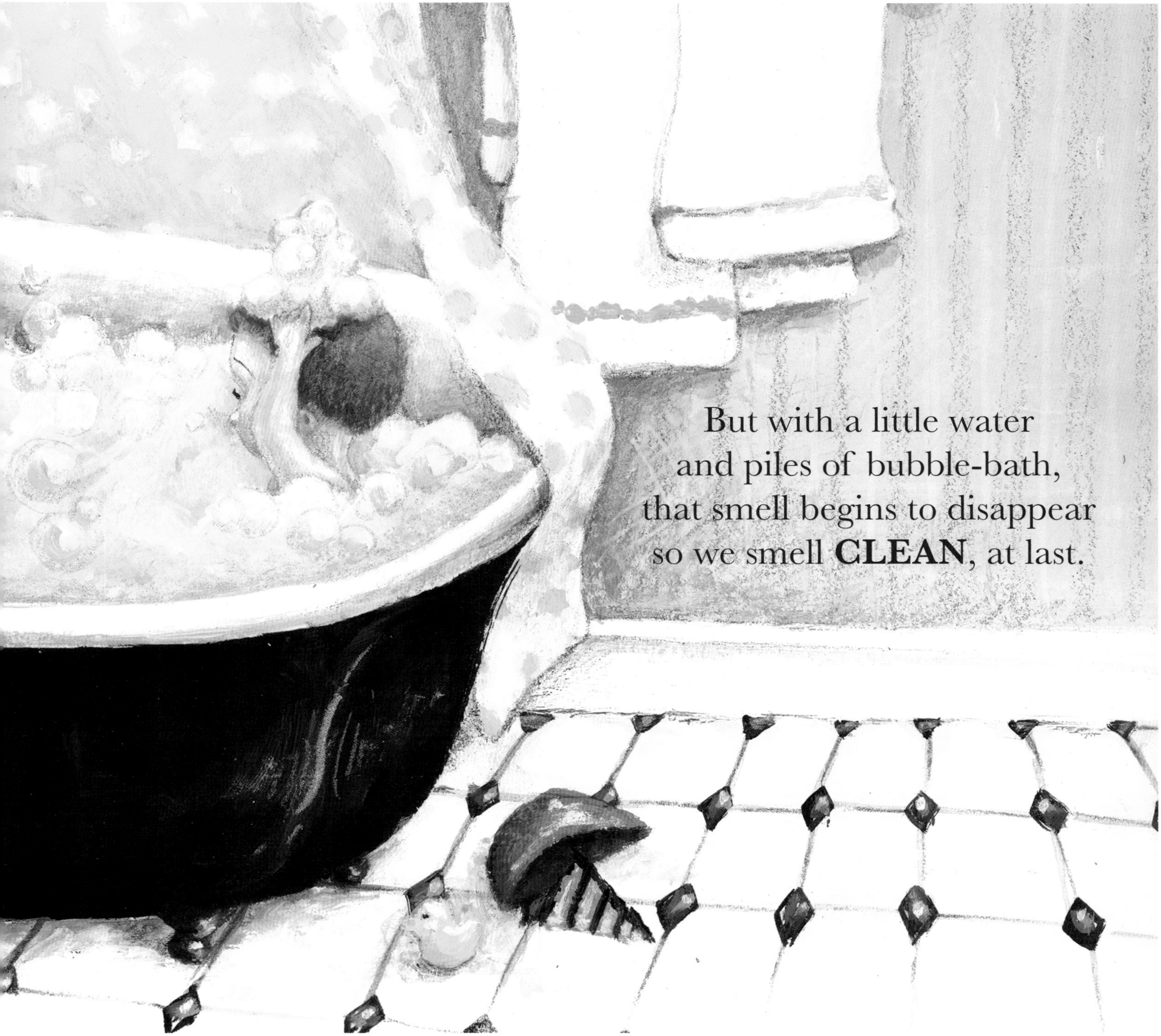

But with a little water
and piles of bubble-bath,
that smell begins to disappear
so we smell **CLEAN**, at last.

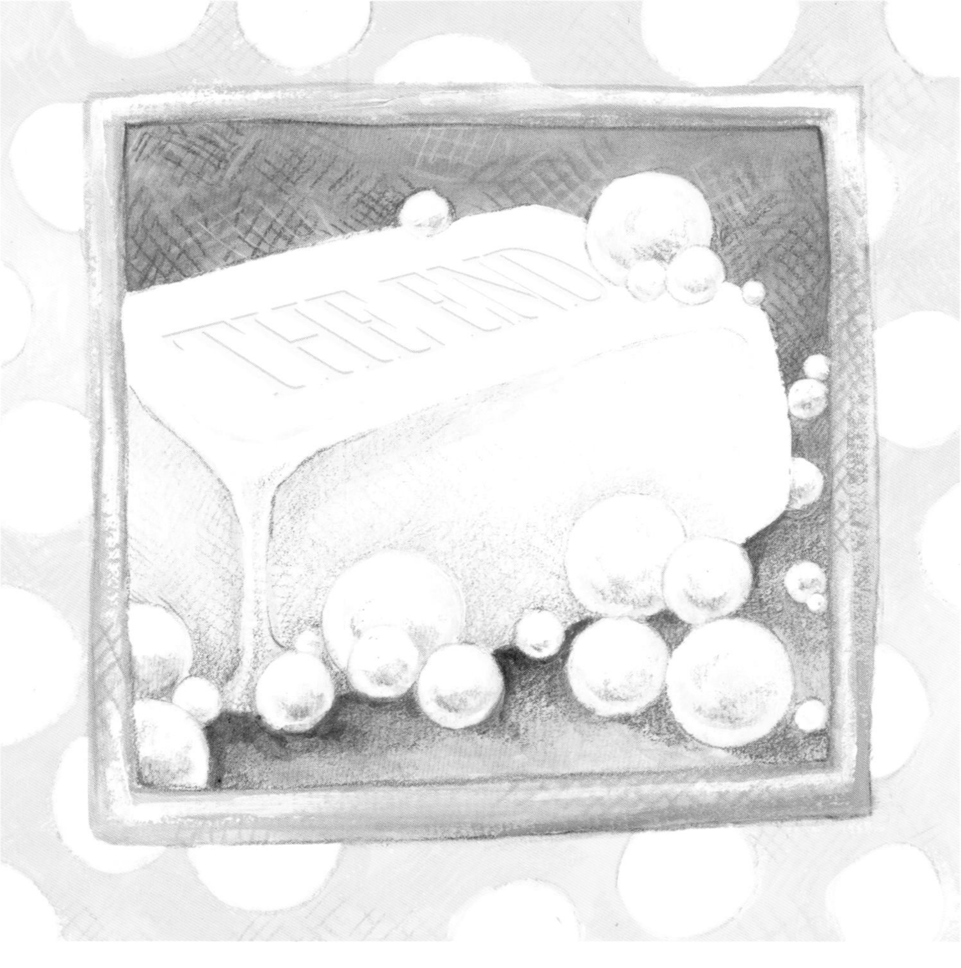
THE END

DATE DUE

OCT 24 '07 S	APR 01 2013	
OCT 17 2007	NOV 18 2015	
FEB 21 '08 S		
FEB 11 2008	MAR 16 2016	
OCT 19 '08 S	NOV 22 2016	
OCT 06 2008	APR 09 2018	
	AUG 29 2022	
JAN 30 '09 S		
JAN 30 2009		
MAR 16 '09 S		
APR 01 2009		
OCT 07 2010		
MAR 15 2011		
FEB 01 2012		
MAR 29 2012		
APR 13 2012		